MW00453694

# BEETHOVEN

## An Introduction to his Piano Works

Willard A. Palmer, Editor

## CONTENTS

K.WoO refers to *Kinsky, Work without opus number.* The number following this designation refers to the number in Kinsky's *Thematisch-Bibliographisches Verzeichnis aller vollendeten Werke Ludwig van Beethovens* (List of all completed works of Ludwig van Beethoven). George Kinsky, a German musicologist, catalogued all of Beethoven's works. He assigned numbers where Beethoven did not write in an opus number. Kinsky's study gives us a chronological listing of all of Beethoven's compositions.

Second Edition

Copyright © MCMXCII by Alfred Publishing Co., Inc.

*Cover art: a detail from the above oil portrait of Beethoven*
*by Joseph Willibrord Mähler, 1804.*
*The Granger Collection, New York*

BEETHOVEN
From the engraving by Blasius Höfel after the drawing by Louis Letronne (1814)
*(Historisches Museum der Stadt Wien)*

BEETHOVEN'S FAVORITE PORTRAIT
*(He had copies made to give his friends)*

# BEETHOVEN

Ludwig van Beethoven was born at Bonn, Germany, on December 16, 1770. He died March 26, 1827, in Vienna. Like most of the great masters, he was a child prodigy and he held several important musical positions at the age of 12. At this time his teacher was Christian Gottlob Neefe, a well-educated musician of high repute. From Neefe he studied harmony and theory and became acquainted with J. S. Bach's keyboard music as well as the works of Handel and many of the Italian and French masters. He also became proficient as a violinist and violist. Beethoven was later to study very briefly with Mozart and for a longer period with Haydn, Albrechtsberger and Salieri. But it was to Neefe that he felt the most keenly indebted for his musical background. When he was 22 years old he wrote to Neefe, "Should I ever become a great man, you will have had a share in it."

Beethoven's initial impact on the musical world was as a brilliant virtuoso of the piano. Those who heard him wrote that his playing was unlike anything ever heard before. His contemporaries were astonished at his "daring deviations from one motive to another,"

his "elemental force" and his "titanic execution." At this time he had composed many works but had not gained much recognition as a creative artist, except for the fact that the musical world of Vienna was amazed at his ability to improvise on any theme presented to him. Because of this ability, he became extremely popular as a performer for the Viennese aristocracy.

Beethoven's growing deafness caused him to eventually withdraw from public life and to devote all of his time to composing. One can trace the growth of his marvelous genius as his heroic struggles with his own infirmities were reflected in his works. His progress as a creative artist was continuous throughout his lifetime, and as he progressed the art of music also progressed. He transformed even such obvious forms as the *theme and variations* into triumphs of musical architecture, and his contribution to the larger forms, such as the *sonata, concerto* and *symphony,* were so profound that they would require volumes for adequate discussion.

Fortunately, Beethoven also found the time to compose a considerable quantity of short piano selections that serve as excellent study material for the young student. In this book will be found some of the most representative of his smaller piano works, prepared from the autographs and/or the earliest editions. Beethoven's original text is presented in dark print, and all editorial suggestions appear in lighter print, with explanations in the footnotes. Through the study of these smaller works as Beethoven actually wrote them, the student can best prepare for the study of his larger compositions.

AUTOGRAPH OF *VARIATIONS ON A SWISS SONG*
Collection of Dr. Hans Carl Bodmer, Zürich
One of the most meticulously written Autographs of Beethoven (1790)

# BEETHOVEN'S LEGATO

According to Czerny, who was Beethoven's pupil, Beethoven's legato was "controlled to an incomparable degree, which at that time all pianists regarded as impossible of execution, for even after Mozart's time the choppy, short, detached manner of playing was the fashion." "Beethoven himself told me," Czerny added, "that he had heard Mozart play on various occasions and that Mozart had accustomed himself to the manner of playing on the harpsichord, then more frequently used, a style in no way adapted to the pianoforte, which was still in its infancy." Beethoven is said to have looked with disdain upon the old Mozart style of playing, which he called "finger dancing" and "manual air-sawing." This may be shocking news to those who have read so much in praise of Mozart's legato, which Mozart himself described as "flowing like oil."

The importance of Beethoven's attitude toward legato playing is emphasized by the fact that he admired Clementi's playing more than Mozart's. He endorsed Clementi's piano method from the moment it became available (around 1803). In this method, Clementi states, "When the composer leaves the LEGATO, and the STACCATO to the performer's taste; the best rule is, to adhere chiefly to the LEGATO; reserving the STACCATO to give SPIRIT occasionally to certain passages, and set off the HIGHER BEAUTIES of the LEGATO." (Capital letters and punctuation are Clementi's.) Such instructions are applicable to the performance of Beethoven's music. Beethoven marked some of his measures with meticulous care and was merciless in his condemnation of any copyist who ignored such markings, or any publisher who printed them incorrectly. On one occasion he insisted that the publisher retrieve all the copies that had been sold to make corrections in them. But many measures were left without indications of staccato, legato, phrasing or dynamics.

In his book, *BEETHOVEN*, Sir Donald Francis Tovey expressed the opinion that, where Beethoven has not made up his own mind, he has not invited editors of his music to make it up for him. Who, then, must decide how such a passage is to be played? As Clementi emphasizes, it is left to the performer's taste. Good music deserves to be interpreted, and the performer should have a share in the creation of it, but such a privilege is only allowable in the light of adequate knowledge of the composer's style and traditions.

In Beethoven's music, many measures are not marked because they are obviously played like similar measures previously marked. In the *Bagatelle,* Op. 119, No. 1, on page 26, for example, the opening phrase is clearly marked, and we may be certain that the following similar phrase is to be played the same way; but the articulation of the notes in measures 5, 6 and 7 are left to the discretion of the individual. With such considerations in mind, it will be obvious which of the editorial indications should be considered to be suggestions (which is one person's opinion of how the music might be acceptably interpreted). On some occasions, these suggestions may save the teacher a bit of time and trouble, and on others they may serve as points of departure.

# BEETHOVEN'S USE OF STACCATO

Beethoven used the wedge-shaped staccato mark (ᵥ) and the dot (·) to indicate different degrees of staccato. In a letter to Karl Holz, in August, 1825, he said, "Where there is a dot above a note, a wedge must not be put, and vice versa---- and are not identical." Clementi, in his method book (1801), which Beethoven endorsed, states that the wedge-shaped staccato mark means that the note should be "released instantly." The dot indicates "a little less staccato." Nothing is said about the wedge-shaped mark indicating any kind of accentuation.

# BEETHOVEN'S USE OF THE SLUR

Beethoven, like Bach, Haydn and the great instrumental composers, used slurs as if they were bowing indications for stringed instruments. When a violinist changes the direction of his bow after only a few notes are played, it is usually for the purpose of effect. The change of bow direction may be used to give a slight emphasis to the first note played in the new direction, as the bow digs slightly into the string. The wind instrumentalist produces a similar effect by "tonguing."

To take a rather extreme example, when the violinist plays the following phrase:

it is bowed as follows ( ⊓ = down bow; V = up bow):

The effect of *separation* between the slurs is not usually intended:

The purpose of such bowing is to produce a slight stress or emphasis on the notes at the beginning of each slur. A comparable effect on the piano might be achieved thus:

(Here we use the dash [—] to indicate an emphasis less than that indicated by the conventional accent mark [>].)

An example is found in the famous *Menuet in G* (page 18) which is thought to have been conceived originally for orchestra and which undoubtedly uses the slur as it is used for stringed instruments:

Ex. 1.

What Beethoven tells us by these markings is that he does *not* want special stress on the beginning of each of the dotted quarter notes in the first full measure, but he *does* want a slight emphasis on the first note of the 2nd, 3rd and 4th measures. These stresses need not all be identical, of course, but should be interpreted with taste— probably with a decreasing amount of emphasis on each one.

Beethoven is also telling us that he *does not* want the more banal phrasing indicated in most modern editions:

Ex. 2.

To the pianist unfamiliar with the traditions of writing for stringed instruments, the desired effect might better be conveyed by the following:

Ex. 3.

The emphasis is *not* on the 3rd count of the 2nd measure and again on the 3rd measure, as the 2nd example implies. Beethoven does use this type of phrasing, however, in the 14th and 15th measures of the selection, further emphasized with *sf*, and much of the pleasing effect of this difference is lost if the opening bars are phrased incorrectly.

In the trio of the same composition, a cross-rhythm, characteristic of Beethoven's style, is revealed in his use of slurs:

 etc.

These slurs indicate a slight emphasis at the beginning of each group of 3 eighth notes. This imposes a feeling of two groups of three per measure against the basic three-beat rhythm of the menuet. The result is characteristic of Beethoven. This effect is completely obscured by the phrasing shown in many modern editions:

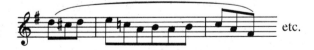 etc.

A similar effect suggests itself in the groups of three notes per measure played by each hand in the 2nd full measure of *Für Elise*, page 32:

 etc.

This effect need not be overdone to the extent of making the last of each group of notes staccato, but the phrasing indicated in some editions results only in a careful and uneventful legato:

Such phrasing also obscures the clever shifts of rhythm employed by Beethoven in measures 12 through 16, as he returns to the original motive:

Could this be a small example of what Anton Schindler, Beethoven's intimate friend and companion, describes as Beethoven's "idiosyncrasies of rhythm" and "accentuation that would not have suggested itself to any other player?"

# MUSIC WITHOUT SLURS

In music for stringed instruments, when no slurs are marked, each note calls for a change in the direction of the bow. The change can be made by a skillful player with practically no break in the continuity of the tone, but the resulting articulation is different than a series of notes played with no change in direction of the bow.

Some of Beethoven's "unmarked measures" are best left unmarked for this reason. As tempting as it may be to the editor to add "helpful" slurs to the opening measures of the *Sonata in G, Op. 49, No. 2* (page 52), it is questionable whether or not they can possibly do anything other than alter Beethoven's intentions, which are made clear by the *absence* of slurs.

The absence of slurs does not necessarily eliminate legato but places a certain importance on the individual notes. This is especially clear in the 3rd measure through the 2nd beat of the 4th measure, where each note needs a subtle emphasis (in proportion, of course, to the length of the note). The only slur this editor feels perfectly justified in adding is one con-

necting the trill to the following note, a slur so obvious that Beethoven probably thought it unnecessary.

The above information should add reason for carefully observing which slurs are part of the original text (those in dark print). If pianists were more familiar with the traditions of violin bowing, Beethoven's piano music would need no editorial slurs at all.

# BEETHOVEN'S ORNAMENTS

In determining the proper execution of Beethoven's ornaments, a few pertinent facts must be considered. As a student, Beethoven was taught to play ornaments in the manner prescribed by C.P.E. Bach. As a teacher, he used C.P.E. Bach's *ESSAY ON THE TRUE ART OF PLAYING KEYBOARD INSTRUMENTS* and Clementi's *ART OF PLAYING ON THE PIANOFORTE*. C.P.E. Bach insisted, as did other 18th century theorists, that all trills must begin on the upper note. Clementi stressed that they generally begin on the upper note but allowed an occasional departure from the rule to preserve a legato with the preceding note. Beethoven was quite aware of the problems that might be created by the allowance of such exceptions and, in passages where there might be confusion, he often inserted a small note indicating the starting note of the trill. In the absence of such a note, we can be reasonably sure that the trill begins on the upper note.

Many music editors insist that, since Beethoven lived in the 19th century, his trills must begin on the principal note. They lose sight of the fact that the trill from the principal note did not begin to come into general use until the publication of Johann Nepomuk Hummel's *COMPLETE THEORETICAL AND PRACTICAL COURSE* in 1828, a year after Beethoven's death.

After Hummel's book was published, many famous artists, including Czerny, who was a great admirer of Hummel, influenced others by playing Beethoven's trills incorrectly. This was not because Beethoven had allowed him to play them in such a fashion. Czerny himself relates that, when he played the *Sonata Pathetique* for Beethoven, the master agreed to take him as a pupil with the proviso that he obtain a copy of C.P.E. Bach's *ESSAY* and bring it with him to the first lesson. We may be certain that Beethoven wanted to point out to Czerny that the trills in this sonata must be played beginning on the upper note.

Only the ornaments used in this book are discussed here.

## 1. THE APPOGGIATURA

All appoggiaturas are played *on the beat*. This is in accordance with C.P.E. Bach, Clementi, and even Hummel.

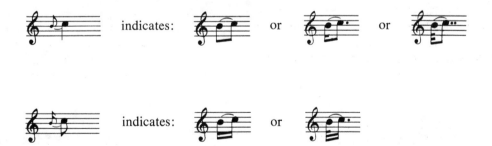

Mozart wrote the sixteenth-note appoggiatura as a small eighth note with a cross-stroke. Beethoven simply wrote a small sixteenth note. In this book we have notated the appoggiaturas as they appear in Beethoven's manuscripts.

♪ is simply an old-fashioned way of writing a small sixteenth note (♬). Such notation does not invariably indicate an appoggiatura that receives less than half the value of the following note. The use of the short appoggiatura is determined largely by the context. C.P.E. Bach, in his *ESSAY ON THE TRUE ART OF PLAYING KEYBOARD INSTRUMENTS*, says that the short appoggiatura is generally employed "before quick notes." In such cases it is "played so rapidly that the following note loses scarcely any of its length." He further informs us that such appoggiaturas may not be identified by their appearance, since they may be written as small eighth, sixteenth or thirty-second notes.

The DOUBLE APPOGGIATURA is also played *on the beat.*

Of Beethoven's own use of the appoggiatura, Anton Schindler wrote, "I may state, as a general remark, that Beethoven gave prominent force to all appoggiaturas, particularly the minor second, even in running passages; and, in slow movements, his transition to the principal note was as delicately managed as it could have been by the voice of a singer."

## 2. THE TRILL 𝆖

All trills begin on the *upper note* unless the *composer* gives some indication to the contrary.

The small notes after the trilled note are used to end the trill and are called the "suffix." These notes become part of the trill and are played with the same speed as the other notes of the trill.

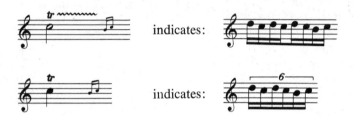

The number of repercussions depends upon the tempo of the composition and the skill and taste of the player. Trills of reasonably long duration are usually played with a suffix, whether the small notes are indicated or not.

## 3. THE TURN ∾

The symbol for the turn may be used as follows:

  a. The accented turn

   In this case, the turn is played *on the beat.*

  b. The unaccented turn

   In this case, the turn is played *after the beat.*

Beethoven occasionally used small notes to indicate the turn. These notes may sometimes be considered a realization of a turn over a note, and sometimes an unaccented turn between two notes.

# BEETHOVEN'S PEDALING

Beethoven is known to have made lavish use of the pedal. Czerny remarked that he used it "far more than he indicated it in his works." The light Viennese piano used by Beethoven during his years of concertizing did not sustain tones as long as the modern piano. For this reason, Beethoven's pedal markings (or the lack of them) cannot serve as much of a guide as to how to play his music on our present instruments. Once again, we are left to our own decisions.

In his autographs, Beethoven used a small circle to indicate the release of the pedal. In printed editions, the indications *Ped.* * have been generally used. In this book we use the more modern indication ⌐_____⌐ which more precisely indicates where the pedal is to be depressed and released.

# BEETHOVEN'S RUBATO

Although many modern pianists have expressed abhorrence at the use of rubato in Beethoven's music, one can be sure that Beethoven used it. Schindler says, "He adopted tempo rubato in the proper sense of the term, as the subject and situation might demand, without the slightest caricature." He also remarked, "Beethoven changed the tempo as the feelings changed."

It seems, from the reports of his contemporaries, that Beethoven did not allow his pupils as much license as he permitted himself. To him it was important that the time be counted correctly, and he admonished many players to "play the music as I wrote it." But this does not mean that he did not permit freedom of *interpretation.* Upon hearing Marie Bigot de Morogues play one of his sonatas, he said to her, "That is not exactly the reading I should have given, but go ahead. If it is not exactly myself, it is something better."

# RECOMMENDED READING

Bach, Carl Philipp Emanuel. ESSAY ON THE TRUE ART OF PLAYING KEYBOARD INSTRUMENTS, W. W. Norton & Co., New York, 1949.
BEETHOVEN: IMPRESSIONS OF CONTEMPORARIES, G. Schirmer, Inc., New York, 1926.
Donington, Robert. THE INTERPRETATION OF EARLY MUSIC, Faber & Faber, 24 Russell Square, London, 1967.
Dorian, Frederick. THE HISTORY OF MUSIC IN PERFORMANCE, W. W. Norton & Co., New York, 1942.
Schonberg, Harold C. THE GREAT PIANISTS FROM MOZART TO THE PRESENT, Simon and Schuster, New York, 1963.
Tovey, Sir Donald Francis. BEETHOVEN, Oxford University Press, London, 1945.

# ACKNOWLEDGMENT

I would like to express my thanks to Judith Simon Linder for her valued assistance in the preparation of this edition.

# ÉCOSSAISE

**Allegro**

K. WoO 23

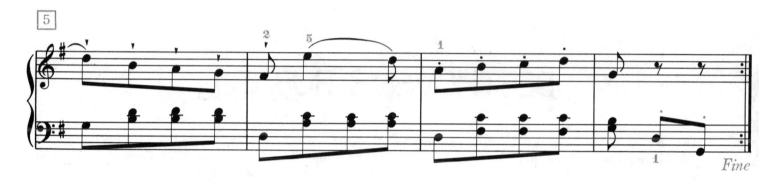

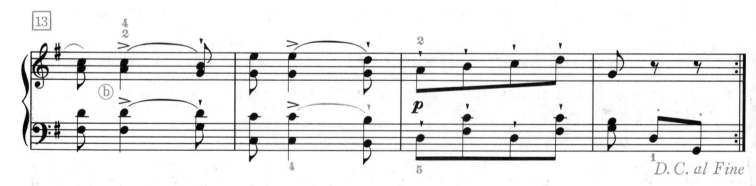

*ÉCOSSAISE*, pronounced "ay-ko-se̲z," is a French word meaning "Scotch." The dance for which the music was composed does not have a Scottish origin, however. The Écossaise was a popular dance in $\frac{2}{4}$ time, usually used for beginning and ending an evening of dancing. Chopin and Schubert also wrote Écossaises, and they are commonly subtitled "Scotch Dances."

The original title of this selection is *ÉCOSSAISE für Militarmusik*. It was composed in 1810 and was published by Czerny after Beethoven's death.

(a) This dissonance was undoubtedly written to be amusing. One can imagine the reaction it may have provoked in Beethoven's day.

(b) The accents should be robust.

# TWO COUNTRY DANCES

**Allegro moderato**

K. WoO 15, No. 1

These two dances are selected from a suite of *6 LÄNDRISCHE TÄNZE* composed in 1802. Beethoven wrote them first for two violins and contrabass and later rewrote them as piano solos.

(a) The *sf*'s in this composition apply only to the right hand.

K. WoO 15, No. 2

**Con moto**

2.

*Fine*

*D.C. al Fine*

(a)  Many editions have **p** here and **f** on the last count of the 4th measure.

# COUNTRY DANCE

K. WoO 11, No. 2

This selection is from *7 LÄNDRISCHE TÄNZE*. It was published both for orchestra and for piano solo.

# LUSTIG, TRAURIG
## (JOYFUL, SORROWFUL)

**Lustig** (Joyful)

K. WoO 54

*il Fine*

It is not definitely known when this selection was composed, but it was probably in the 1790's. It was not published until 1888.

**Traurig** (Sorrowful)

*Da Capo* (Lustig)

# MENUET
## IN C

K. WoO 10, No. 1

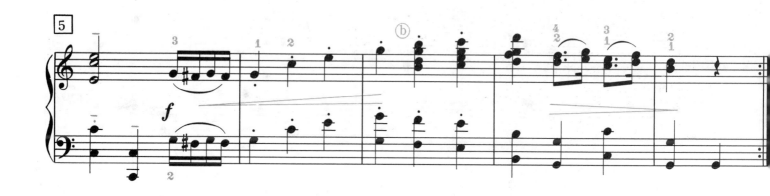

*Fine*

This and the following two selections in the book are from *6 MENUETTEN*, composed in 1795.

(a)  In this and similar places the slur in dark print, from the original edition, does not imply a break before the first count of the next measure. See page 4.

(b)  For a simplified version, the lower note of each of the three chords may be omitted.

**Trio**

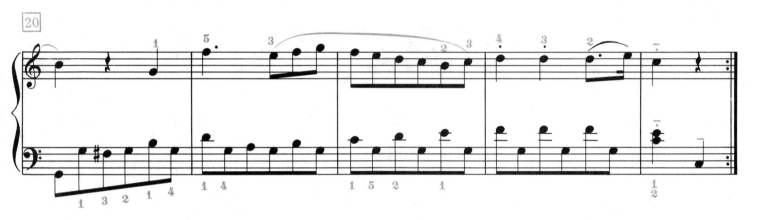

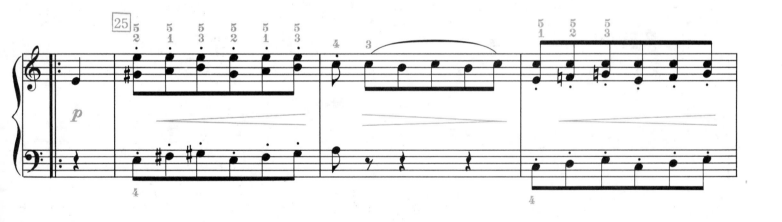

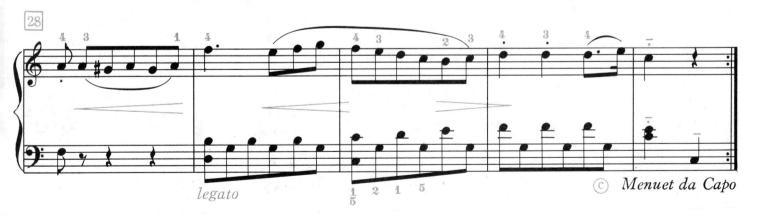

Ⓒ *Menuet da Capo*

Ⓒ  Play the Menuet from the beginning to the Fine, without repetitions.

# MENUET
## IN G

K. WoO 10, No. 2

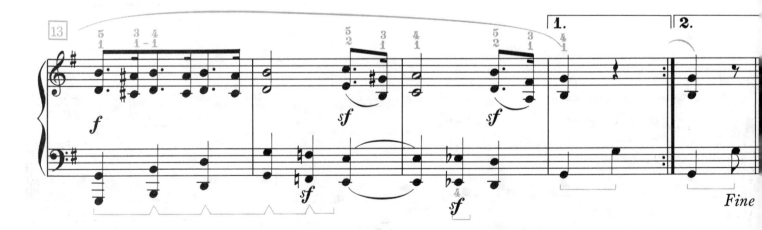

*Fine*

(a) No break in the legato is intended by the separate slurs. The notes should be smoothly connected from the beginning to the first quarter rest. See the discussion of the function of the slurs in this selection on page 5.

**Trio**

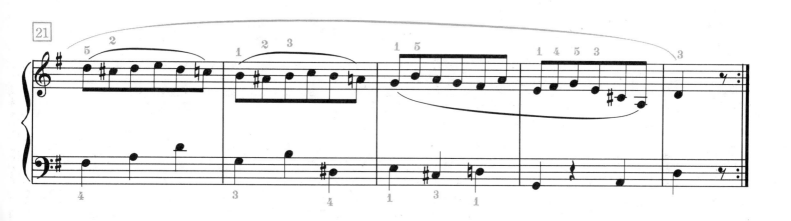

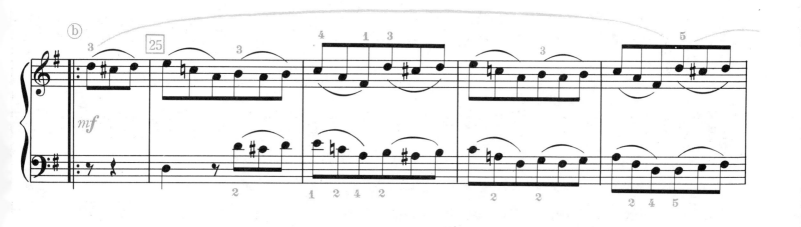

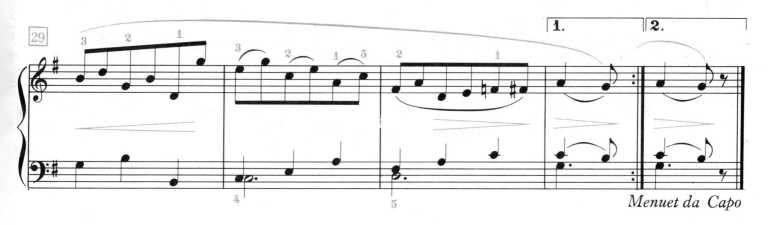

*Menuet da Capo*

(b) Special attention is directed to the slurs. See the discussion on page 5.

# MENUET
## IN D

Moderato e maestoso

K. WoO 10, No. 5

*Fine*

a) Pedaling is optional. Beethoven indicates none.

*Menuet da Capo*

ⓑ *fp*'s apply to the upper note, which must be struck with sufficient force to be heard for its full duration.

# SONATINA
## IN G

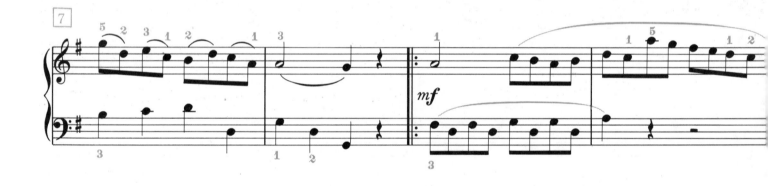

No number has been assigned to this work.

(a)  This appoggiatura may also be played thus:

(b)  In this and similar places no break in the legato is intended—only a slight emphasis on the 1st note of the measure. See page 4.

24

**Romanze**

a) The chords are broken from the bottom upwards, beginning *on the beat*.

*a tempo*      *come prima*

*legato*

b)   The ornament may also be played thus:

# BAGATELLE

Op. 119, No.

Allegretto

(a) Most editions have the following phrasing:

This is, of course, not indicated by Beethoven, and the performer must decide which phrasing he prefers.

(b) The turn is given as shown in the autograph. In both of the first editions it stands between the A and C and could be realized:

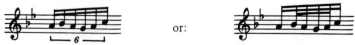

or:

(c) The wedge-shaped staccato marks, differing from the ordinary dots used in the opening measure, are found in both of the first editions and in the autograph. See the discussion, BEETHOVEN'S USE OF STACCATO, page 4.

d) The text here is given according to the autograph and the Clementi
edition. The Schlesinger edition has:

(e)     The wedge-shaped staccato marks are found in both of the first editions but are missing in the autograph.

(f) Most editions show all notes staccato in measures 55 through 65. The slurs in light print emphasize the shift of rhythm so characteristic of Beethoven's style. No perceptible break should be made between the slurs, but a slight emphasis should be given the first note of each group of four.

(g) Our text here is according to the first edition and the Schlesinger edition. The autograph has a quarter rest on the first count of the measure and the G on the second.

(h) The arpeggiations appear in the first edition and in the Schlesinger edition, but not in the autograph. They were undoubtedly added by Beethoven.

# BAGATELLE

À l'allemande

Op. 119, No. 3

(a) Most editions have [musical example] . None of this phrasing was indicated by Beethoven. He probably wanted a legato, but with each note played clearly and distinctly. See the discussion MUSIC WITHOUT SLURS, page 6.

(b) The lowest note in this chord is scratched out in the autograph but appears in the first edition and the Schlesinger edition.

Da capo fin' al segno 𝄋
ed allora la Coda

Coda

(c) Beethoven's Italian is translated literally as follows: "From the beginning, ending at the sign 𝄋 , and then the Coda."

(d) The lowest note of the chord is missing in the autograph but appears in the first edition and in the Schlesinger edition.

# FÜR ELISE *

K. WoO 59

**Poco moto**

(a) In most modern editions, this note appears as a D instead of an E (here and in subsequent similar passages). In the original edition and in the only known Beethoven autograph sketch, the note appears as an E throughout the composition.

\* This work was originally published with the title *Clavierstück in A moll* ("Keyboard piece in A minor"), but the autograph bore the title *Für Elise am 27 April 1810 zur Erinnerung von L. v. Beethoven* ("for Elise on April 27, 1810, as a remembrance of L. v. Beethoven"). The autograph has been missing since 1867, when the piece was first published.

(b) The turn does not appear in the original edition.
If it is observed, the measure may be played thus:

(c) Here the original has f' instead of e'. Our text agrees with the more modern editions.

(d) All notes in this and the following two measures were originally written in the upper staff.

(e) Pedal indications are from the original edition. On the modern piano it may be more effective to break the pedaling at the beginning of each measure and omit it during the chromatic passage beginning at measure 82.

# THEME FROM RONDO A CAPRICCIO
## (RAGE OVER THE LOST PENNY)

ⓐ **Alla ingharese, quasi un capriccio**

Op. 129

The *Rondo a Capriccio* has been a favorite with concert performers for many years. It was left unfinished by Beethoven and was probably completed by Diabelli, who published it in 1828. The autograph is in a private collection in Providence, Rhode Island, and it reveals many differences from most published versions. The measures shown on these pages are taken from a facsimile of the autograph. Editorial suggestions, as usual, are in light print. The complete title, thought to have been added by Anton Schindler, is *"Die Wüth über den verloren Groschen, ausgestobt in einen Kaprize"* (Rage over the lost penny, vented in a caprice).

ⓐ *In gypsy style, like a caprice.* The word "ingharese" combines *ongarese* (Hungarian) and *zingarese* (gypsy).

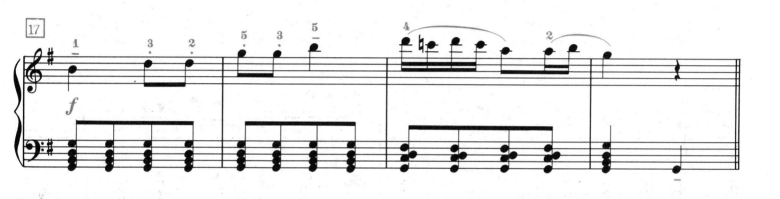

(b) The trill may be played with more repercussions.

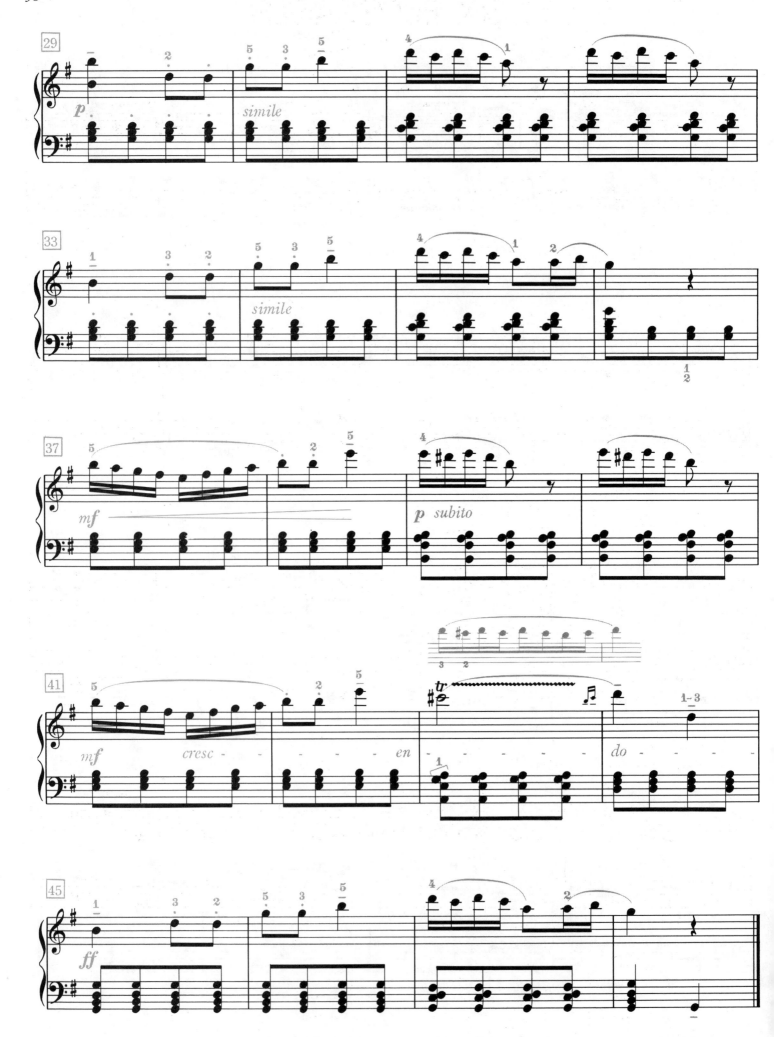

# SIX ÉCOSSAISES

K. WoO 83

The *SIX ÉCOSSAISES* are intended to be performed as one selection. Each part should be taken at the same tempo, with no interruptions between the parts.

(a) No *forte* appears here in the original. Perhaps this is an oversight. The dynamics indicated by this editor offer some relief from the monotony of playing this theme *forte* at each entrance.

(b) See the discussion of THE TURN on page 8.

(c) The decision as to whether these notes should be legato, non legato, or detached is left to the individual. See pages 3 and 4.

# VARIATIONS ON A SWISS SONG

K. WoO 64

A facsimile of the autograph of the first page of this selection appears on page 3.

The theme should be played boldly but simply. The most brilliant execution should be reserved for the last variation. Crescendi and diminuendi may be added at the discretion of the individual. Beethoven indicated none.

(a) The fingering in dark print is from Beethoven's original manuscript.

ⓑ  Beethoven's directions are clear. The entire variation is **𝒑** and legato. The slurs serve the function discussed on page 4.

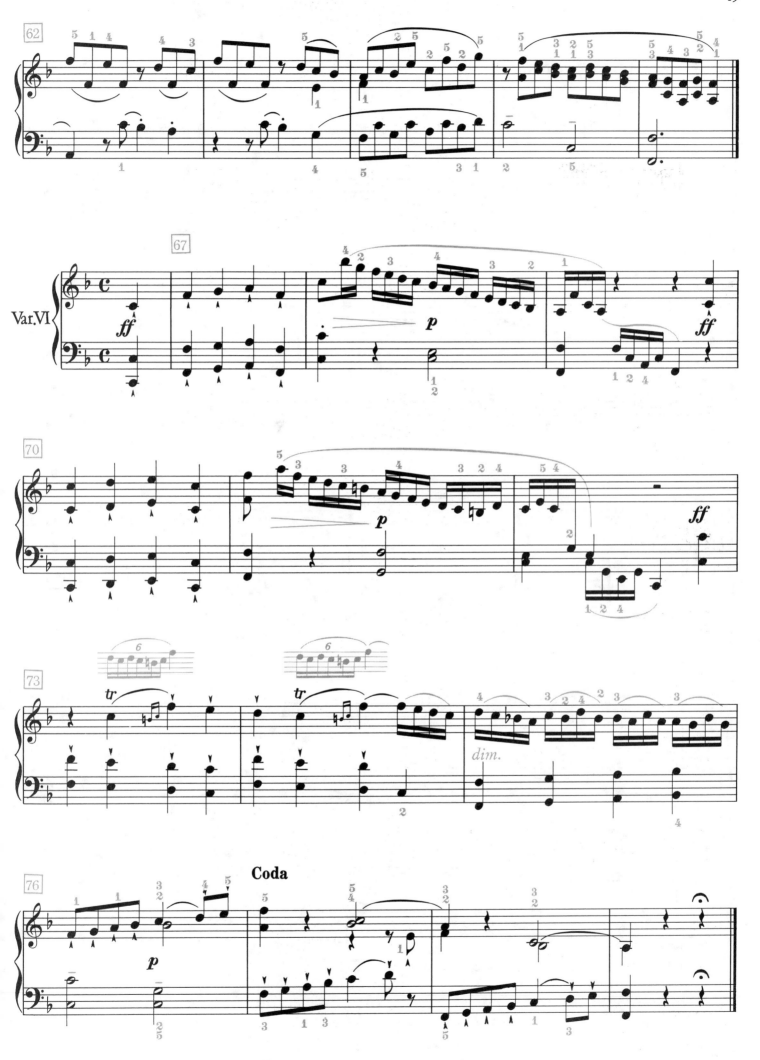

# BAGATELLE

Op. 119, No. 2

Andante con moto

ⓐ    All pedaling in this selection is optional. Beethoven gave no pedal indications.

ⓑ  Both the first edition and the Schlesinger edition show the final note as it appears above.

The autograph, however, has

# SONATA
## IN G

**Allegro ma non troppo**

Some teachers may prefer to have the student learn the 2nd movement first, since it is the easier of the two. Either movement may be played as an individual selection, of course.

(a)  See the discussion of these measures on page 6.

(b)  Pedaling is left to the discretion of the performer. Beethoven indicated none.

 This trill does not have a suffix in the original edition. The use of the suffix here has been established in the 4th measure, which is identical. As a general rule, the suffix is played when the trill is long enough to accommodate it, whether it is indicated or not. See page 8.

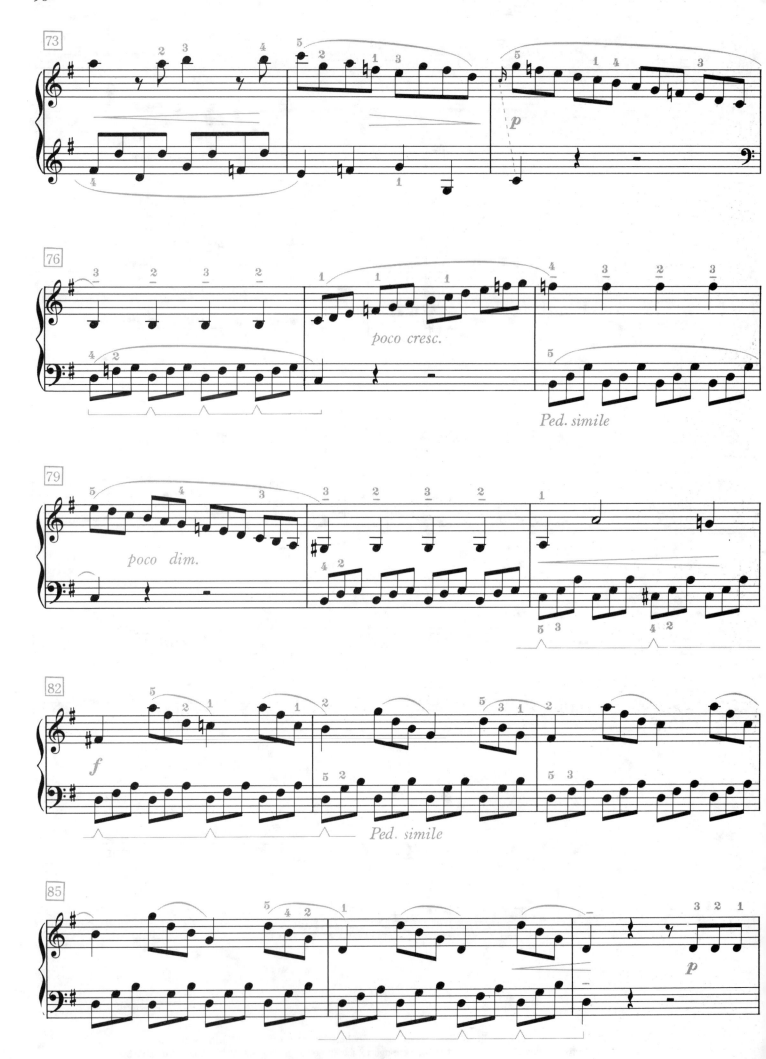

**Tempo di Menuetto**

poco staccato

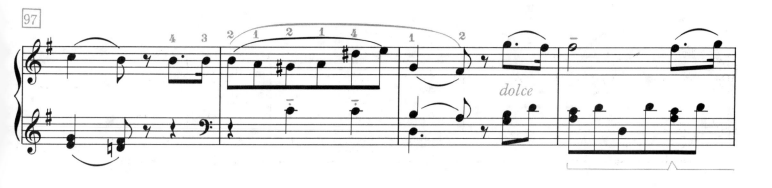